Your Destiny
awaits you!...

Carolyn Jacob

The Secrets of the Everlasting Kingdom

CAROLYN LACEK

Written and Illustrated by
Carolyn Lacek

Published by:
Grace Ministries International, Inc. (GMI)
d/b/a Jubilee News
P.O. Box 86
Monessen, PA 15062

http://.graceministriesglobal.org

ISBN: 978-1-7376284-2-2

First Edition
Printed in the U.S.A.

This book is dedicated to
The Glorious Prince,
The One and Only
Dream Come True,
and to His precious
Princess, the object
of His love and affection.
May they live happily
ever after.

~*~*~*~*~*~*~*~*~

With special thanks
to my faithful loving
husband David
and to our beautiful
daughters Katelyn
and Angelina.

I am so grateful for all of
their love and support.

TABLE OF CONTENTS

FORWARD

The book you are holding is not just a picture book or a storybook, but a timely, inspired work from Holy Spirit given to Carolyn Lacek who has been open to insight, revelation and supernatural downloads and uploads from God.

I have known Carolyn for a little over five years and she has a wonderful generational family heritage of artistic gifting that God uses to its fullest to relay His heart to His children. "Secrets of The Everlasting Kingdom" is a Heavenly Visual Expression released from her innermost being where her God-given gift is seated, and it's being published for the season we are now in -- a New Era -- for such a time as this.

The spiritual value of this work cannot be measured by earth's standards because the words recorded in this book along with the illustrations carry an impartation of revelation for your life. It will awaken that which is sleeping within that may be holding you back from Destiny's Purpose for your life. With that being said, I emphasize this is no ordinary book. I know, because I read, and I too experienced.

As the anointing of God awakens your innermost being with Truth, you will receive a visual understanding of the Love that Father God, Jesus, and Holy Spirit have for you. I capitalized the word "Love" because the Love of the Father has nothing to do with the love that comes forth through our human nature. The Love of the Father proceeds out of HIS nature, moving through us to others. In this Love is the ability for us to be used to our fullest through Holy Spirit to make an eternal difference in people's lives thanks to Jesus. It's a Love that can be experienced here on Earth NOW.

As you read and your eyes are anointed to see in a new way, light will fill you to overflowing and you will come to understand on a deeper level who the Trinity is and who you are in God's infinite plan. You will be given a "relatable peek" from Heaven into the much larger picture that you are a part of.

I urge you to lay down any expectations of what you think this book may be. The intense beauty of this book is that... yes, it is a tale, but not a fictitious one. The definition of a tale is *"a fictitious or a true narrative, especially one that is imaginatively recounted.* God's creative breath is upon this "Masterpiece" because it is the "Master's Piece" (Peace) created just for you. It's been His heart all along for you to see and comprehend who He is and who He made you to be in His Kingdom.

If you are in a place of discouragement, I encourage you to go into a quiet place and read this book. Be strengthened in Jesus' Name!

I encourage anyone who is a parent to read this as a bedtime story to your child. Not only will you train up your child to know the Love of the Father, but God will strengthen your own spiritual walk with Him as well.

Think it not a coincidence that you are holding this book in your hands right now because it is Father God's Gift to you, His son and daughter -- an Open Heaven experience -- that will enable you to grasp the width, length, depth, height, and the magnitude of Jesus' Majestic Love for you, His Bride. As you read and take in this one-of-a-kind Love, it will bring change where change is needed; it will add to you whatever was lacking, and will penetrate unreachable places that you knew nothing about. This glorious tale is God's *"tool to pull"* you closer to Him in ways you never imagined possible.

I end with a quote taken from this tale: *"The writings inside this book will give you an understanding of your true identity and the magnitude of all that has been bestowed upon you. You must then share the secrets with all of mankind."*

I declare you will see with new eyes, the Love of Jesus and Holy Spirit emanating out of the Heart of the Father, as well as the magnification of HOW they move together in Destiny's purpose.

You are here with great purpose, and you will come to know who you really are. You will come to know that you are on the mind of Father God every second of the day!

Get ready! This is your time for Destiny to be Awakened! You will never be the same!

Appreciation of the Mystery

"For this reason I bow my knees to the Father of our Lord Jesus Christ, from whom the whole family in heaven and earth is named, that He would grant you, according to the riches of His glory, to be strengthened with might through His Spirit in the inner man, that Christ may dwell in your hearts through faith; that you, being rooted and grounded in love, may be able to comprehend with all the saints what is the width and length and depth and height — to know the love of Christ which passes knowledge; that you may be filled with all the fullness of God".

-Ephesians 3:14-19 NKJV-

In HIS Love and mine,

Hazel K. Palmer,
President and Publisher
Jubilee News
Grace Ministries International, Inc. (GMI)

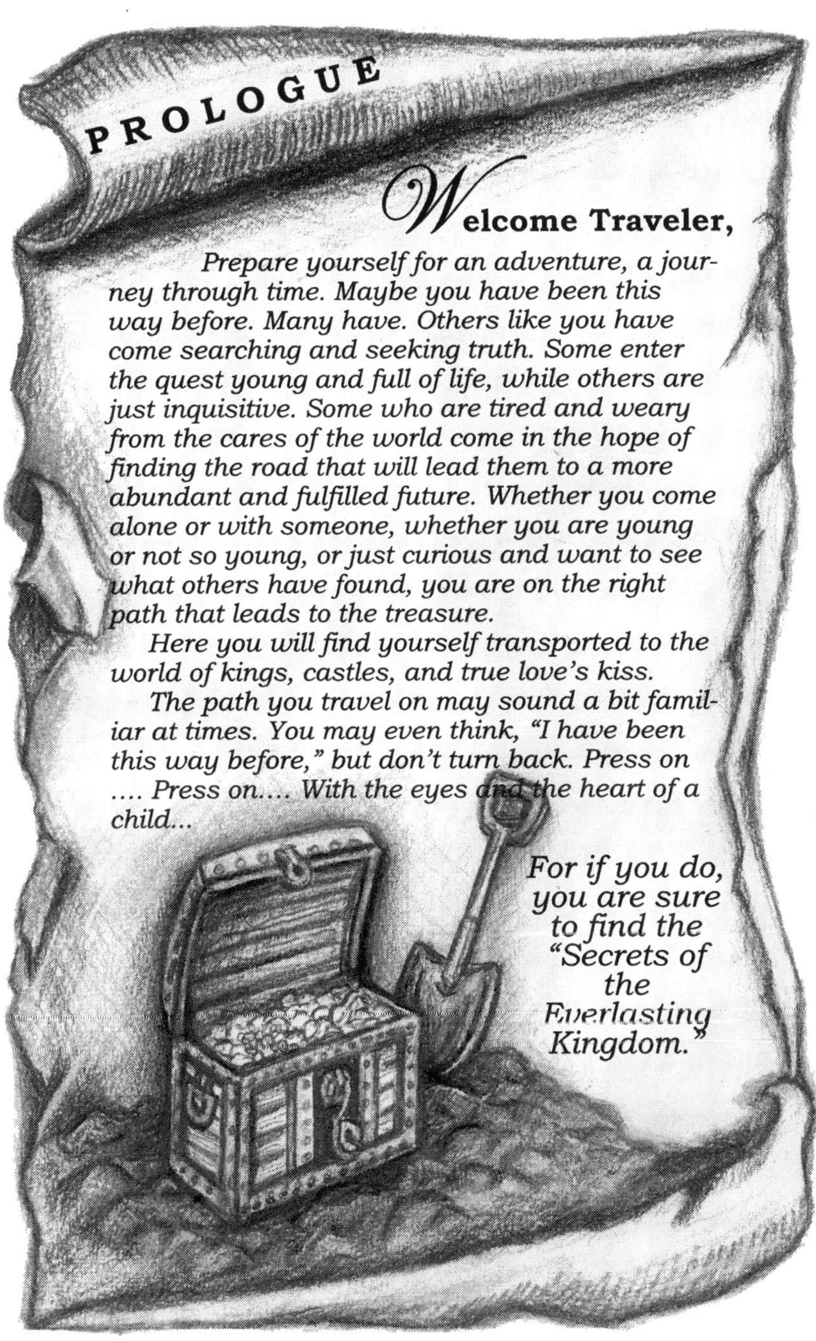

PROLOGUE

Welcome Traveler,

Prepare yourself for an adventure, a journey through time. Maybe you have been this way before. Many have. Others like you have come searching and seeking truth. Some enter the quest young and full of life, while others are just inquisitive. Some who are tired and weary from the cares of the world come in the hope of finding the road that will lead them to a more abundant and fulfilled future. Whether you come alone or with someone, whether you are young or not so young, or just curious and want to see what others have found, you are on the right path that leads to the treasure.

Here you will find yourself transported to the world of kings, castles, and true love's kiss.

The path you travel on may sound a bit familiar at times. You may even think, "I have been this way before," but don't turn back. Press on .... Press on.... With the eyes and the heart of a child...

For if you do, you are sure to find the "Secrets of the Everlasting Kingdom."

Far FAR Away and a very long time ago, in the Everlasting Kingdom that always was and ever shall be, lived the magnificent and glorious King Elohim, the Ancient of Days. His Kingdom was like no other, for it was as vast as the expanse of the universe, and His subjects as numerous as the countless stars in the sky. The streets leading to the castle were paved in shimmering gold, and the celestial angels sang in His courts night and day.

King Elohim had a beloved Son, who pleased Him greatly. No father ever loved his son more than King Elohim loved His. His Son, Emmanuel the Great, would one day be known in all the kingdoms that exists, by an even more exalted title. He loved His Father in return with all that was within Him and even as His Son, Emmanuel served the King with devotion and loyalty.

Being the Wisest of all Wise, the King finally decided that the time had come for Prince Emmanuel to find the Bride with whom He was meant to eventually share His Kingdom with. This meeting would require much planning and preparation because the Prince would have to enter a land where time exists in a way that was much different from His Kingdom. This is because time in the Everlasting Kingdom was not, and never shall be, like time as we know it. For in the Endless Kingdom, a thousand years is like a day, and a day is like a thousand years. It was in this realm, that King Elohim finally summoned the Prince to come before Him.

The Prince respectfully entered the Throne Room and knelt before the King. With a smile, the King spoke, “Arise, Emmanuel, and come sit beside Me.”

He paused for a moment while the Prince sat down on His own throne at His Father’s right hand. “My beloved Son,” King Elohim continued, “I am sending You away to another kingdom.”

“Mankind?” asked the Prince, raising his eyebrows thoughtfully.

“Yes, Emmanuel, “the King continued to explain. “As You know, the land where time exists is in a dimension quite different from this glorious one, but still very beautiful. You will live among the sons of man and become one of them for a time. You shall come to know them and love them in a different way than You have been able to here, because You will be in human form. Many of them will return Your love, but not all. Some will even become Your enemies, and plot against You.”

"I see," said the Prince. "What would be the purpose of My journey?"

"It is there among all humanity that You will meet Your Bride. Her exceptional beauty will take Your breath away, and You will love her with all that is within You. Her destiny shall not only be to reign with You in Our Kingdom one day, but to unite the two kingdoms together forever." Then King Elohim paused a moment and the Prince waited expectantly.

"However, I must warn You of the perils of this extremely dangerous mission. Many things shall You suffer because of Your love for her and all mankind. The Prince of the Power of the Air will be sure to come against You with all his might, and a fierce battle will follow. It will cost You everything, but because You will crush the head of that deadly serpent, Your Bride to be will live forever, and her entire kingdom will ultimately be set free from the power of his control." The King looked at His Son, "So now that you know the importance and the purpose of this mission that only You, Son of Elohim can fulfill I have only one question. Will You go?

The Prince looked directly and purposefully into the King's eyes. "I will go, Father," replied the Prince without hesitation.

And so, with His Father's blessing the preparations were made and the Prince left for His journey. He then set out on His brilliant white stallion reach the spiral staircase of time. The Prince would descend this staircase into the foreign kingdom to become one of the sons of man.

Two angels accompanied the Prince as He set out on His journey from the palace to the spiral staircase. It was dusk now, and the air was filled with a cool, fine mist. The two angels flew before Him, carrying glowing torches to light the way. By the time they reached the staircase, a dense fog had set in around its entrance. Through this hazy atmosphere, the Prince dismounted His horse and waved goodbye to the angels as He prepared for His final departure.

-The Spiral Staircase-

The Prince stepped out of the fog at the very door to the staircase and paused to look at the entrance of the radiant structure He was about to descend. Its sides were a beaming white light filled with the full colorful spectrum of a glorious rainbow shining through it. Each step going down was clear, like a sheet of glass. The staircase itself traveled down so far that He could not see the last step at the end far below from up here at the intriguing first step of its entrance. The two curious angels with Him stayed close at hand, peering down through the fog to watch the Son of Elohim prepare to descend.

He proceeded to take His first transforming step over the threshold to begin His descent down the staircase leading to another dimension. Not only were the steps translucent, but with each step His foot alighted, He peculiarly became . . . a little younger! It was quite apparent to the angels that something unusual was happening to Him. “He’s beginning to shrink!” the first one exclaimed to the other.

“Oh no . . .” responded the other one, astonished, “He . . . He is getting younger! Look . . . He’s turning into . . . a young lad! ”

By the time they looked at each other and then back at the Prince, He had traveled down the staircase even farther, and was gaining speed. Faster and faster, He descended until He was no longer able to walk! He now had to crawl as an infant to continue down the glassy steps!

“We must help Him!” said the angels to each other in a panic, and they flew down hoping to assist Him. But when they reached Him, He had become . . . a newborn baby, lying on the very last step! They stooped down to pick Him up, when suddenly the Prince disappeared altogether!

“What has happened?” they cried to each other. “Look!” The first one spotted a tiny seed laying upon the step where the Prince had been lying. Suddenly, there was a brilliant flash of light, followed by a loud, resounding clap of thunder that shook the staircase. Out of nowhere appeared a glowing white dove in flight. It alighted just long enough to pick up the seed in His mouth and fly away.

to

"What does this mean?" the second angel asked looking puzzled.

"He has crossed over to the other kingdom..." the first angel reflected. "He is ready to become one of them."

The Prince Returns

Thirty years or so passed by in the Kingdom of Mankind, but only moments passed in the Kingdom that Always Was and Ever Shall be, when suddenly a great sound of trumpets filled the air. "The Prince has returned!" a glorious chorus of angels chanted. The triumphant sound resounded throughout the land.

"My Lord, the Prince has arrived," announced the seraphim.

"Send Him in!" the King replied. He could hardly contain the overwhelming sense of pride and admiration He had for His Son. He already knew the agony of the sacrifice the Prince had made and was anxious to welcome Him home. The Prince entered the Throne Room and knelt respectfully before the King. "I have returned, Father," He stated bravely. His voice full of emotion. "The deed is done."

The King stood to His feet, prepared to honor His Son in a dignified way, and said, "Arise, Emmanuel." As His Son stood to His feet, the somber King was no longer able to hold back His own overwhelming feelings. He threw His arms around

His Son in a loving embrace, and both wept together for a very long time.

The King finally managed to compose Himself and speak. "I see Your wounds are very deep, Emmanuel."

"Yes," replied the Prince as He also was coming out of the impact of that highly charged moment. He cleared His throat and went on to express His feelings. "As deep as My love for her, Father. These scars are the marks of My love that brought the Princess to life. I have seen her, and I know that she is the one meant for Me. Even more than this, My scars will remind Me and all who look upon them, that those who live in the land of time can now be free from the tyranny of Beelzebub, if they believe and understand all that was done for them."

Then the Prince took a deep breath and went on to explain.

"I must tell You also of My love for all of mankind. My time with them was priceless to Me, but there is so much that they do not understand." The King nodded wisely, for He was able to identify with His Son's emotions.

"The day is coming when the Princess will finally fully comprehend all that You have done on their behalf. She will understand and be able to lead them in truth, but she will never know the full pain You withstood to deliver her and her kingdom," said King Elohim.

"It is as it should be," the Prince replied, His eyes again fighting back the tears.

King Elohim then turned and summoned the seraphim to enter His presence. The angel handed the King His sword. Suddenly the room was filled with a heavenly host of angels who had all rushed in to witness this supreme and regal ceremony. A tentative silence fell upon the assembly as they anticipated this long- awaited announcement.

"Kneel, Emmanuel," The King said. He touched His sword to His Son's shoulders, knighting Him. As He did so, small bolts of lightning emerged from the sword and attached themselves to the Prince. These electrifying bolts produced a brilliant glow of white light, which engulfed the Princes' body, resting upon Him.
Then the King continued, "Let now the Royal Proclamation go forth: From this day forward, My Son Emmanuel the Great, shall be known as Emmanuel the Sovereign Prince of Peace. A low rumble of thunder responded in awe to the magnitude of this barrier breaking decree.

The King paused smiling slightly, amused by the thunder's reply. Then He continued addressing His Son directly, "Every knee shall bow to You Emmanuel, in the Everlasting Kingdom, the Kingdom of Mankind, and the kingdom of the evil one." Again, the thunder voiced its approval, this time a bit louder and longer. As soon as the thunder settled back down, King Elohim continued His edict. “All honor and power and authority now rests upon You, Emmanuel, from this moment forward and forevermore.”

At this last statement, the heavenlies shook, as the roar of thunder applauded King Elohim’s announcement. The assembled host of angels burst into an exuberant chorus of praise. Then what appeared to be thousands and thousands of tiny sparks went shooting forth from the lightning bolts. They had emerged from the King’s sword and were plunging downward creating trails of stardust-like particles behind them. These sparks were newly created beings whose sole purpose was to go forth from the Everlasting Kingdom and enter the land of time. There they would echo the King’s Eternal Proclamation to all those among men who had ears to hear.

The King went on to further give accolades and respect to His Son.

“Your authority and power are the legacy of Your Bride also. She is in her infancy now, and even as we speak, a dispatch of angelic visitors is arriving to deliver gifts for her at a dedication ceremony in honor of her arrival.”

The Royal Dedication

Far below in the Kingdom of Mankind, within the realm of time as we know it, a great celebration was soon to begin. Destiny, the newly born heiress to the throne, was about to be dedicated to the Kingdom of Mankind by her proud parents. The King and Queen of the land of time had been unable to have a child of their own, and for many years had earnestly prayed for this day to come. With joyous anticipation, everyone took his seat at the grand banquet table as the royal proclamation was about to be read.

"Hear ye! Hear ye!" cried the grand duke. "Your majesties the King and Queen announce the birth and royal dedication of their newborn daughter, Princess Destiny, to the entire Kingdom of Mankind which lies within the realm of time as we know it." There arose a great applause from the assembled guests, for many were thrilled to finally behold their newborn Destiny.

The King then stood up and said "We are honored by your presence this day as we assemble to witness the royal ceremony, and the bestowing of gifts upon our daughter. Arrangements have already been made for the betrothal of Princess Destiny to the Sovereign Prince of Peace, Emmanuel, from the Everlasting Kingdom that Always Was and Ever Shall be. His Father, the Omnipotent King Elohim, has sent to us an entourage of angels to present His invaluable gifts to our Destiny.... And so, without further ado, let the angels come forth!"

Great thunderous applause filled the air as six glorious, winged creatures appeared before the crowd, each carrying an ornate pitcher in hand.

The first angel holding a golden pitcher adorned with rubies hovered over the tiny baby's cradle. "I give to you the gift of loving grace," said the angel. "Destiny will become graceful as she learns to extend grace and mercy in purest love to others in the same measure it has been given to her." As he spoke, he tilted the pitcher, pouring forth a substance like crimson colored dust trickling down through the air, lighting upon the tiny Princess. Where it touched the newborn babe, it was gently absorbed into her skin.

The second angel came forward with a golden pitcher embossed with purple amethyst. "I bring the gift of leadership. Destiny shall lead her people well with power, authority, and honor," the angel announced as he poured out glittering particles of deep royal purple amethyst dust. The next angel stepped forward holding a lovely pitcher arrayed with amber stones. "Serving," he said. "With the heart of a servant-leader, Destiny shall learn to serve her people well," declared the angel as golden dust that shimmered in the light was sprinkled out upon her.

A pitcher trimmed with emeralds which was presented by the fourth angel, contained the gift of giving. "Destiny shall increasingly give of what she has, and what little she has shall be made more."

said the angel. The infant, sleeping peacefully, was enveloped in the sparkling emerald dust.

The sapphire covered pitcher carried by the fifth angel poured out the gift of wisdom. “Destiny shall be wise beyond her years, and truth shall be illuminated to her with increased understanding,” he said as he tipped his pitcher over the infant.

The sixth angel came forward carrying a golden pitcher ornately garnished with grayish-brown agate gemstones. “Destiny shall be clothed in the gift of true humility,” he said. “She shall always know whose power and authority she carries and to whom all honor truly is due.” Everyone present stood in reverent silence, captivated by what was transpiring in their midst.

The Evil Proclamation

Suddenly, the room began to shake. Then an ominous cloud of black smoke appeared before them, in the center of which stood the fallen angel, Beelzebub, ,the wicked Prince of the Power of the Air. The crowd cried out in fear and anguish, as the sinister creature advanced and pointed his bony finger in the King's face.

"So...," sneered the evil Prince. "I see all around me that the whole kingdom has turned out for the celebration ceremony on behalf of the Princess. I suppose my invitation got lost in the mail . . . Is that so, your highness?"

"J-just a . . . little oversight, Beelzebub," the King stammered. "W-would you like a piece of cake?"

"Si-lence!" bellowed the dark Prince. "Don't patronize me!" Then he calmed, and after a moment, continued in a sickly-sweet voice. "Well now, let us not let a little oversight cause any hard feelings. I, too, have a gift for this Princess of little Destiny." As he smugly stood holding forth his staff, he proclaimed to the crowd.

"Destiny shall indeed grow in all the gifts she has received, but when she has reached the age of maturity, and the plan for her life is about to be fulfilled, she will prick her finger upon the needle of a spinning wheel . . . and die!" With these words, black smoke once again appeared, engulfing the dark intruder. Then just as quickly as he had come and interrupted the majesty of the moment... Beelzebub was gone!

The crowd gasped in and horror. Fear and panic began to arise in the room as the words of the dark Prince of the Power of the Air echoed in their minds.

Just then, arriving late to the banquet hall came another glorious, winged creature holding a golden pitcher embellished with glistening diamond studs. The angel hurriedly approached the thrones of the fear stunned couple. “Forgive me for the timing of my arrival your Grace,” the angel said addressing the King. . . I was delayed,” he explained.
“Your timing is just right,” whispered the angel holding the amethyst pitcher, urging him to make his proclamation in hopes of changing the atmosphere in the room. “Make haste and announce your gift! Beelzebub just spoke a curse over Destiny, with a sentence of death! He doesn’t want to see her united with the Prince,” the late arriver was informed. “Your gift will bring them hope.”

This last angel stepped forward. “Your Majesty, there is one more gift to be presented to the Princess . . . ”. It was difficult to hear the angel’s voice because of the uproar in the crowd.

“Silence!” the terrified King demanded. All the guests quieted down and quickly returned to their seats, obeying his command. “Proceed” nodded the King to the angel wit the diamond pitcher.

“Thank you, your Majesty.” The angel took a deep breath before he continued. “In the name of Elohim, The Sovereign Ruler of all the Universe, I bring the gift of prophecy.”

“Not only is this gift bestowed upon her, but

the first prophecy shall be about her." After a tense moment heightened with anticipation, the angel went on to proclaim the prophecy. " Destiny shall not die on that fateful day she pricks her finger on the spinning wheel. The power of death has already been broken on her behalf , and this dear King and Queen, cannot be changed. She will only fall into a deep sleep until true love's kiss awakens her from her slumber."
Then the angel poured out the glistening vessel containing the sparkling diamond dust upon her.

Unfortunately, even though these words should have been a great comfort and relief to the King, Queen and all the people, the wicked last words of Beelzebub had already begun to take root in the hearts of the people. As a result, the angel's proclamations were heard, but not received by the crowd. They had all already become overwhelmed by the deadly curse of Beelzebub. Whisperings and mutterings filled the hall, and the seven angels from King Elohim watched them for a moment in sadness.

Then seeing that thcy had done all that they had been commanded to do by King Elohim, the celestial beings departed from the banquet hall, and returned to the Everlasting Kingdom.

The King and Queen, realizing that the angels had left, hastily dismissed the rest of their guests too and returned to the throne room. There, they gathered their chief advisors and counselors to discuss this grave threat, concluding that the matter had to be handled immediately. So, in order that no unfortunate accidents should ever occur in the life of the Princess, the King decreed that all the spinning wheels in the kingdom were to be destroyed. Even though the king had received them as a gift from King Elohim, he felt this had to be done. To do this, the king sent forth the proclamation to destroy the spinning wheels. Immediately upon releasing the proclamation he dispatched his soldiers to perform the enormous task of gathering up every spinning wheel to be brought to the castle and burned. None one of the leaders in Mankind consulted King Elohim or the Prince on this matter. Rather, they tried to hide the whole incident from them and handle it in their own strength.

The Window of Eternity

Of course, in the Kingdom that Always Was and Ever Shall Be, the Ancient of Days, the Wisest of all Wise, already knew what had taken place. He stood before the Window of Eternity peering down at what was happening in the realm of time below. "Will they ever learn?" the King sighed sadly to Himself. "Will they ever learn?" He repeated, shaking His head, watching the frantic scene below awhile longer. His heart was filled with compassion for them. How He longed for them to trust Him. With tears in His eyes, He called to the attending seraphim, "Send for My Son!"

Moments later, Emmanuel appeared in the Throne Room, with a look of expectation upon His face.

"What is it Father?" He asked.

"I am deeply troubled concerning what I am about to show You," said King Elohim. "Mankind has again lost its way in a cloud of deception which has suddenly overshadowed them." With a wave of His hand the Window of Eternity opened wider to reveal again the scene of Princess Destiny's dedication. Emanuel saw the gifts being given, the evil curse that had been proclaimed by Beelzebub, and the crowd's reaction. Grief filled His heart as He too saw that they had completely failed to grasp the hope of restoration contained in the last angel's prophecy.

Then someone caught Emmanuel's eye, a child whose face was cupped in her hands was crying out to the Sovereign of the Everlasting Kingdom. "Who is that small lass weeping in the corner of the room?" asked Emmanuel finally. "That is little Faith," explained the King.

"I hear her crying, 'Please, come rescue her! Come help us, Prince Emmanuel,'" noted the Prince.

The King walked away from the window and sighed. Prince Emmanuel followed silently. "It is because of Faith that I will send You to help them. She will grow in wisdom and maturity, and one day become Your Bride's constant companion." A moment later, He continued. "The royal counsel of man has decided to confiscate all of the spinning wheels in the land and burn them, because they are so afraid."

"Spinning wheels . . ." the Prince said, shaking His head in disbelief. "Mankind's useless attempt to take matters into their own hands." Nodding His head in agreement, the King spoke,

"Bring Me the book," As King commanded, one of the seraphs in the attending assembly of angels responded and quietly left the room. After another moment of thoughtful silence, King Elohim continued. "I am sending You back down to them on a quest to rescue the Princess, and her kingdom. You will not travel through the staircase this time, but You will make Your way on a wave of My Spirit. This will not however be the appointed time to bring Your lovely Bride home to Us. You will visit her in her ill-fated slumber, and Your kiss will bring life back to her and revive all of their land." He went on to explain, "The whole kingdom will be so deceived by the words of Beelzebub that they shall all eventually fall asleep. Your visitation shall undo the bewitching spell and foil Beelzebub's destructive plan." Prince Emmanuel nodded excitedly, but King Elohim was not done speaking.

"Now, My Son, let Me show You Your Destiny as she has become. She has grown into a beautiful woman, and I want You to see the precious jewel that awaits You." With a wave of His hand, the Window of Eternity near them slowly revealed the form of a stunning, young Princess. She was adorned in regal robes of purple and fine tapestry. Her long, shimmering, dark hair reflected light from the sun, and upon her head was a golden crown adorned with a single red ruby. Her soft, brown eyes enhanced her beautiful face. Her lips were a deep crimson red, and the sound of her laughter was like music. The Prince stood gazing at her, entranced, until finally He spoke, "She is incredible." His Father smiled, watching His Son's reaction.

"Far more lovely than her appearance is her character, My Son. All who have come to know her praise her for this."
"What is she doing?" asked the Prince, watching her.

"At this moment she is playing Hide and Seek with the children of the servants of the palace," answered the King.

"Father," said the Prince, very amused by what He was watching. "I remember that game. I played it when I was a youth. Can't I leave now? I would love to hide and have her come seeking after Me," He said, His eyes still riveted upon her.

"There will be plenty of time for lovers' games later," chuckled the King. "Besides, the game You are viewing now will soon come to an unhappy end. This is the point in time that Destiny unknowingly will fall into the enemy's trap." The King lifted His hand again, and the view of Mankind revealed through the window began to fade.

The Prince had a lump in His throat. " Nevertheless. I'd like to see." He said knowing He would not rest until He was aware of her fate.
The King looked thoughtfully at His Son and said, "If You wish, My Son, but it will be painful for You to watch." The Prince nodded soberly.

Elohim waved His hand again before the window.

A vision of Princess Destiny climbing a long staircase to an unused portion of the castle began to take shape. At the top, she found an old forgotten door to a storage room that nobody had used in many, many years. Thinking she had found the perfect hiding place, the Princess crept inside. A large window, as well as the fact that she forgot to close the door behind her, kept the room well lit.

Many old things had been stored inside. One item of particular interest though to the Princess was an object she had never seen before standing in the corner of the room. She began to move toward it for a closer look. An eerie presence filled the room, as a dark, shadowy figure had now appeared behind the Princess. It enticed her to move forward towards the intriguing device.

Recognizing the presence of evil, and the lure of the spinning wheel, the Prince cried out, "No! Don't touch it!"

The Princess, walking toward it, stopped in her tracks as she heard a voice cry out in her heart, "Don't touch it!"

She paused a few seconds, then being beckoned forward by the evil force continued towards it anyway, thinking, "What harm could it do to examine this closer?"

Destiny stretched forth her arm towards the spinning wheel, first turning the wheel and then touching its spindle. Within seconds, she had pricked her finger on the needle of the spinning wheel and was lying on the floor unconscious.

The Prince turned away from the window, His eyes shut and His teeth clenched. His hand was in a tight fist over His heart, just above the great scar.

"What must I do to go to her?" asked the Prince in great emotional pain. The King put His hand upon His Son's shoulder to comfort Him, and said, "I will speak to the Great Paraclete. He shall be traveling with You. Go now and prepare Yourself for the journey, but before You leave, I want to give You something to take to her."

The Secrets of the Everlasting Kingdom

The angel who had left previously at the command of King Elohim, returned with a book bound in gold with precious stones set in embossed pink roses upon its cover. As the King nodded toward him, the angel handed the book to the Prince. Emmanuel read the title aloud, "The Secrets of the Everlasting Kingdom." Then He noticed a keyhole under the title. "Is there a key to unlock this book?" asked the Prince.

The angel handed the Prince a white linen sash, and Emmanuel unfolded it. He then found a pocket hidden on the back of it containing two large keys tied together with a scarlet ribbon. There was a word engraved on each copper key. One said "Surrendered" the other "Obedience."

The King explained. "Anyone can unlock this book using just one key, but to unlock its secrets they must use both. I have been writing this ancient book for all those living in the realm of time since the origin of man. Some in the realm of time have gotten to read the uncompleted version, but I purposed not to finish recording its secrets until after Your return from battle and Destiny's birth.

It is finished now. There are no other writings like it. These archives will explain the mysteries of Our oneness with the Paraclete, and many other secrets of Our Kingdom to her and all those in the land of time who will use both keys to open it. Without this book as their guide, the true meaning of life for them will be distorted. These deceptions will lead men astray, and Beelzebub will overtake them. When they read all that has been recorded here, they will have a better understanding of Our Sovereign Kingdom. The Princess must realize who she really is, and to what throne she is truly an heiress. She will finally comprehend the personal suffering You endured to give her life, and what she represents to all of mankind. Present this treasury of truth to her after she has awakened."

"I will," said the Prince while tying the white sash with the hidden keys around His waist. "Thank you," He said as He hugged His Father with deep admiration. Then He began to leave the Throne Room, when suddenly He stopped in His tracks and turned back to His Father.

"You know, it just occurred to Me that a kiss brought about My death, and a kiss shall bring her back to life." Reflecting upon this truth that led to triumph in His previous journey, Emmanuel then left, carrying the book containing the secrets to His Kingdom that He would give to His Beloved.

The Devastating Discovery

It took a while for the children of the palace to find the Princess lying in a deep sleep on the storage room floor. The King and Queen were notified of this tragedy and hurried to her side, accompanied by her dearest friend Faith. She had grown into an accomplished young woman herself and was now the Princess's closest companion. She reminded the grief-stricken parents about the prophecy that the last angel had given at Destiny's dedication, that she would only sleep until true love's kiss would awaken her. Nevertheless, the despondent King and Queen had her dressed in white silk and laid on a blue satin bed in her chambers. Day after day they sat by her side, calling her name, holding her hand, and hoping for a change in her condition, but nothing happened.

At times, the Princess tossed and turned in her sleep, seeming to be quite disturbed, but still her parents could not bring her back to consciousness. They simply could not know the dreams she was having. These were not merely meaningless illusions in the night, but glimpses of events, that had happened in past, present, or were to come.

The Recurring Dreams

The same sequence of events seemed to happen to Destiny as she lay sleeping, a captive audience of one of the truths revealed over and over again in dream imagery. First, a scene would appear of a bride wearing a crowned veil and beautiful white gown, accompanied by her groom, who was also adorned in a majestic crown and wearing a sparkling white wedding garment. Together they stood before a staircase, revealed by a parting in the clouds before them that seemed to reach into the heavenly sky above. The groom was directing her attention to the top of the staircase where a gate made of clouds opened before them. As the gate opened, behind it a city would start to materialize, out of the clouds and mist and shimmering particles that came out of nowhere. She never saw the faces of the elusive pair in this night vision, but something about them seemed familiar. Then suddenly, before the bride and groom could climb the staircase before them or explore the City of Paradise, the awe-inspiring scene would end. Still reeling from its splendor and beauty, Destiny struggled to wake up. Yet each time found it impossible. She could however ponder in her subconscious what she was viewing. She wondered who the couple was and what awaited them behind the city gates.

All too quickly, a dark but no less profound dream began to take shape. She would repeatedly find herself shifted into a much more puzzling dream full of tumult and dread.

Shadows of cruel soldiers beating a prisoner held bound in chains began to take shape in this second dream. The sound of jeers and sarcastic laughter filled her ears as they pushed and spat upon the fallen man. They forced him to carry a large log that he could scarcely drag along, because loss of blood had made him so weak. Again and again, she caught a glimpse him falling, his body groaning in pain from all his open wounds. All she could think of was how much she wanted to help him but could not. She was part of an angry crowd that was pushing and straining to catch a better look at the tortured prisoner as he went by. Her princess robes had disappeared, and she was dressed as a commoner, just like everyone else that surrounded her.

"Who is that man, and what has he done?" she finally asked in anguished desperation of one of the men in the crowd.

"How is it that you do not know? How could you not have heard? He is the one who said He was the Son of King Elohim. Do not worry though; they are going to take care of Him! He's been sentenced to death and is on His way to the cross right now," explained the man from the crowd. He sounded very pleased with himself, that justice was being served to a criminal. Yet what more had the bound man done other than admit who he was?

Suddenly Destiny found herself in front of

the vengeful mob with a ladle of water in her hand. She did not know how she had gotten there. It was as if some unknown force had thrust her forward. At that moment, the battered man fell again, and He was now within reach of where she was standing. Impulsively, she stepped forward to His side, and as she did so, it was as if time stood still. No one came to stop her. All the noise from the crowd and the shouting of the soldiers seemed to be silenced. The ladle of water in her hand now had a purpose. She could give Him a drink!

The innocent victim looked up at her. As she knelt to offer Him the ladle of water, she lifted His head with her hands. In that moment, the amazed princess saw her own reflection in His eyes, and a loving expression upon His face. She did not expect to see this, especially from someone amid such torture. She was so startled by this that she gasped and dropped the ladle, splashing water all over the ground between them. At that instant, the spell of silence began to break, and a soldier came and roughly grabbed the man and stood Him back to His feet, then pushed Him to continue His tortured journey.

In a voice of hatred, the soldier shouted at her, "Get back!"

All the noises from this fiercely angry crowd returned in a tidal wave of sound washing over her, and her frozen moment of time with Him was over. Even so, still she could not move from where she was kneeling. With tears in her eyes, she looked down, horrified at her own reaction to the man. She had not been able to give Him one sip. Then she noticed the blood that was on her hands, blood that came from the wounds on His head. She began to cry as she looked back up to see Him once again as He stumbled down the road. He stopped and turned briefly to look at the one who meant to help Him once more. He smiled at her, and then the soldier pushed Him on as the crowds swirled suddenly between them again, erasing her view.

Suddenly the Princess realized that she had recognized His face. A few years ago, while playing in the castle courtyard with the children, she had wandered off and came upon the castle well. She had idly looked down into the well as she drew herself a drink from the bucket and noticed something very odd about her reflection. Staring back at her from the water was the reflection of herself adorned as a bride, with a handsome stranger dressed like a prince standing beside her!

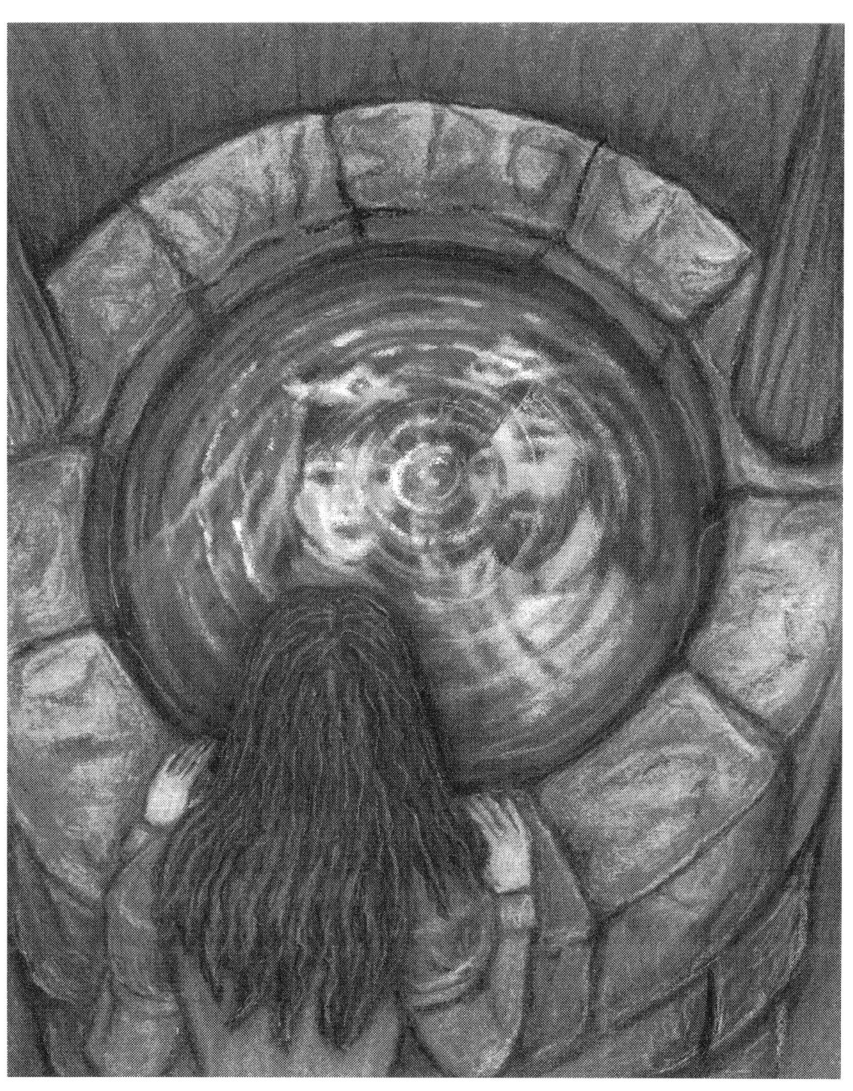

This ill-treated prisoner that she had just tried to help looked just like the man in her vision in the water of the well. Could this be the one that she had been told about her whole life? Was this the great sacrifice that people said He had made on her behalf? She had been told about this so many times she did not pay attention to it too much anymore. In fact, she secretly was resentful and angry with King Elohim for arranging this royal betrothal between their two kingdoms, turning away in her heart from wanting anything to do with it. Now the dilemma of what she saw in her dreams, and the anger against Elohim made her toss and turn. Was this the great Prince to whom she was to marry? How could these things be?

The reality of all that she had seen in the dream began to affect her and impact her heart in deep and remarkable ways. Nevertheless, even as she reflected on all she saw in these two dreams, the Princess Destiny slept on and on, dreaming the dreams, and some others with similar themes that weave a thread of a message she could not grasp, again and again.

The Curse Continues

The day upon which Destiny fell into her accursed slumber, a dark, gloomy cloud appeared over the castle and slowly spread out to cover even the outskirts of the kingdom. As the days went on, turning first into months and then years, the cloud grew thicker and darker with every passing day, eventually plunging the entire kingdom into almost total darkness.

The Princess's heartbroken parents could no longer bear the anguish of what they saw happening. As the weight of dark depression seemed to overtake the kingdom, they too came under the spell of the wicked Beelzebub and eventually fell asleep also. Beautiful, young Faith tried all along to keep their spirits up, but despite her efforts, she never was able to undo the power of the curse spoken that evil day. Seeing finally that even the governing forces of mankind had succumbed to the evil spell, Faith herself was eventually weakened also. In time, she finally allowed herself to give up the fight against evil too and joined her rulers in their despondent slumber.

Across the land, the news that the King and

Queen had been overtaken by the powerful spell brought fear and depression upon all the people. Now knowing they had also lost Faith, in total hopelessness, they all lied down and fell into each their own deep, and endless sleep.

In time, great thorny briars grew up, completely surrounding the castle. Their branches like tentacles grew swiftly, becoming thicker and wider. The immense briars eventually had overtaken the castle so completely, that only its tallest tower remained just barely visible. Beelzebub, anticipating the Prince's rescue attempt, wanted to do everything in his power to keep Him away from His sleeping beauty. The Dark Prince also sent fierce giants armed with clubs and javelins to inhabit the dark and deadly forest he had grown.

Through many years, the Princess slept on, along with her parents, servants, and staff, behind the deep wall of briars that had grown around them. Only the one who loved her beyond measure, with no thought for Himself, would ever be able to rescue her and the other sleeping captives.

Finally, the appointed hour came and the Prince was prepared for His journey. He climbed on the back of the Majestic and All-powerful Paraclete. They left in a flash of white light on the invisible wave of the Spirit, and entered the realm where time exists, to revive Destiny and all that was hers.

The Valiant Rescue

Moments later, they came upon the great thorny stronghold cloaked in darkness around the distressed castle. In that same moment, as They entered the realm of time, Beelzebub became instinctively aware of the aura of Their presence. Upon turning toward the direction of the castle, He saw the light, which surrounded their glorified bodies. Beelzebub immediately sent his strongest demonic forces to attack the courageous Prince and His Noble Companion. Thousands and thousands of eerie deformed spirits flew towards Them out of the pitch-black night, determined to obstruct Their vision. The spirits bombarded Them to cause the Prince and Paraclete to crash into and become painfully impaled by the thorns of the great briars. Despite this horrendous attack, their menacing efforts were to no avail. In response, the brave Prince, riding on the back of the Holy Avenger, spoke into the darkness to the thorny fortress.

"You strongholds of the evil one,
I curse you to death!"
declared the Prince.

As He spoke, His words became as a glowing sword that attacked the imprisoning briars with incredible force. They instantly were cut back, creating a wide path before the Prince to fly through. The layers of briars behind the ones that were touched by the sword began to shrivel up and die too, until within minutes, every last ranch of the captured fortress had withered and fallen away. The grip of deep darkness began to ever let so slightly go, as the smallest hint, of early morning light started to emerge.

Within these minutes, the dark, menacing demons became paralyzed with a fear of their own by the fire they saw in both Emmanuel's eyes and those of His Winged Accomplice. Their evil haven of rest had been destroyed. They could only manage to slither away like snakes in terror, for They knew then that They were powerless to defeat this Invincible Team.

The defiant band of giants then decided to join the fray and mount an overwhelming attack against Them. Combining their forces, these hideous brutes lunged forward from the shadows trying to dismount the Prince from the back of the Almighty Paraclete and tear Him limb from limb.

Aware of their sinister plot, the Prince spoke with authority into the darkness, the simple and powerful words, “Be gone!”

The loud sound of His voice echoed like the sound of many waters, and the ground underneath them shook uncontrollably. Within seconds, every one of the huge creatures disintegrated each one into its own separate pile of black ashes. The Great Paraclete quickly drew a large breath, from the depths of His being. Then He released a mighty wind, which blew upon the ashes scattering them in all directions, until not a trace of dust was left behind. Beelzebub had been watching what was happening as he cowered in the night under some nearby weeping willow trees. In humiliated despair, he realized that he was unable to stop this Valiant Team even using all his special forces, and he was left to face this conflict alone. As he remembered his previous battle with the Prince and his ultimate defeat, his head began to throb in pain, and he trembled in fear to the core of his being. Without another thought, he fled too, dragging his tail behind him, for he was not willing to do direct combat with the Son of Righteousness again.

At last, having overcome all the obstacles set before Him, Emmanuel dismounted in front of the great castle door hanging ajar. The rusty hinges of the heavy iron door creaked loudly, as He pushed it open. His eyes opened widely as He, beheld an astonishing sight. Scores of seemingly lifeless people lay sleeping, everywhere, illuminated only by the aura of light, which surrounded the Prince. The servants, chief advisors, and the royals were all simply lying about, deeply unconscious to His presence. He saw that even Faith was lying powerless among them. Huge cobwebs hung from every corner, even draping down over the sleeping victims. He pushed them aside as He cautiously stepped over the bodies and climbed the tower to the Princess's chamber.

The Glorious Awakening

Quietly, The Prince opened the door to the bedchamber and found His beloved lying therein on her satin bed. The moment of their meeting had finally arrived. Light from His own face fell across her ashen features. He paused a moment as He looked at her. Then finally He spoke.

"Awake, My Destiny," He whispered to her, while gazing upon her beauty. Then He tenderly kissed her lips.

Moments later, her eyes fluttered, and she began to stretch. Outside, dawn began to break, and light trickled into the room.

Color came back into her pale cheeks, as slowly her eyes opened. Astounded that she was finally awake, she found herself starring into Emmanuel's handsome and wonderful face. Then all at once she realized she was looking into the face of her one true love.

Immediately she remembered the dreams that she had dreamt for so many years while she slept. She recalled the great sacrifice she had witnessed repeatedly and all that had been done on her behalf, and for the sake of the Kingdom of Mankind. Although she saw the pain that had been inflicted upon Him, she had never felt it, and knew she never would.

Then all at once she remembered the previous dream she always had. As she recalled the celestial scene, the opened gates, and the elusive couple. For the first time in her life everything began to make sense.

Finally, Destiny was able to speak. “I know who You are,” she admitted at last. “I have been dreaming about You.” She reached for His hand, then drew it back in fear when she saw the great scar upon it.

"The marks of love," He said, aware of what she was looking at. "... I will wear them always."

"Yes," she said blinking back the tears. "... I know. I can't tell You .... I am so sorry.... How can I express...," she stammered, trying to complete her thoughts, but she could not, because she was too choked up with guilty feelings and deep sorrow.
"All is forgiven, Destiny; be at peace," He said in a calm and soothing tone, taking her hand. At the very moment He touched her, an overwhelming peace came upon her, and all anxiety left her.

Then not knowing what else to say, she asked, "... How did this happen to me?"

Emmanuel did not hesitate to explain. "At the celebration of your birth, you had bestowed upon you great gifts that were sent to you by My Father King Elohim. Suddenly the Prince of the Power of the air appeared and deceived the people of the kingdom. "

"Beelzebub" ...,she stated knowing all about what happened that day. "Why does he hate me so much?"

"A very long time ago before your kingdom existed, Beelzebub was an exquisite creature in My Father's house with many special privileges. He turned on the King and led many angels away to create his own kingdom. He fell from the heavenlies with all his own followers, and they became hideous beings. Their only thought is to lead more and more astray using every means of deception and destruction they can. Ever since then, he has hated anyone connected with my Father and Our kingdom. Mankind, and you are especially he despises because you are the one meant to be My Bride," Emmanuel explained.

The day of your dedication a great fear came upon mankind, They believed the dark prince's words that you would die when you pricked your finger on the spinning wheel. This of course, could not happen, My love, for I had already conquered death for you. You are immortal now and will live forever." Destiny's eyes widened, as she could scarcely comprehend such a thing as being real. Additionally, His dark piercing eyes were too much to look at, so she turned her head away to break eye contact with Him.

"You must believe Me," the Prince said. A lump began to form in His throat when He saw her reaction. " Many things you do not understand right now, but you must trust Me. It is true," He said.

Destiny looked back at Him and finally nodded her head sheepishly and smiled. She would put her trust in Him because she could feel His love for her. It permeated the atmosphere.

"I have brought you something that will help you understand." He took her hand and helped her to her feet. "It is an invaluable treasure prepared for you by My Father." As soon as He finished speaking, a dazzling bright light chasing away every shadow or hint of darkness, filled the room. Through it, the familiar form of a great winged being began to take shape. The Princess drew back behind the Prince, a little afraid of the enormity of the wondrous Paraclete. "Are you afraid of Him?" said Emmanuel.

"Yes," whispered the Princess shrinking back. "I

remember Him from my childhood. I didn't understand His power or His ways, so I stayed away from Him. After a while, I didn't see Him anymore. I thought He was gone forever."

"No," replied the Prince, "He was still there. He just withdrew Himself because of your reaction. Do not be afraid of Him. He has accompanied Me today to free you from the thorny fortress that held the kingdom captive. You see, after you touched the spinning wheel, you fell into a deep and endless sleep. The prophecy given at your dedication said you would not die, but only sleep until true love's kiss could revive you. That is why I am here today. I have awakened you, and now you must awaken your entire kingdom."

"My kingdom?" she asked, astonished at the thought.

"Yes," He responded. "After a long while of trying to revive you themselves, the king and queen, in deep despair, hopelessly fell asleep also. Then across the land, hopelessness spread like a plague, until everyone throughout the kingdom eventually fell asleep. Beelzebub then sent great thorny briars to cover the castle. He has done everything he could do to keep Me away, but to no avail, for still I am here."

The Prince reached up between the downy soft wings of the Almighty Paraclete, and took down the ancient-looking book, before presenting it to her. Then, as quickly as He came, the beautiful, large being disappeared, His form swallowed up in the bright light that vanished before them. Fascinated, the Princess examined the gold bound book laden with precious stones and embossed pink roses on it.

"The Secrets of the Everlasting Kingdom," she read aloud. Then she noticed the keyhole underneath the title. "How do I open it?" she asked. Emmanuel took the white sash from around His waist and handed it to her.

Turn over this sash, and you will find a hidden pocket," He said. The Princess turned over the sash and found the two hidden keys tied together with scarlet ribbon. She read the inscriptions, "Surrendered" on one, and "Obedience" on the other. "You may open the book with just one key, but you will need to use both to unlock its secrets," the Prince continued, repeating His Father's instructions. "Wear the sash around your waist with both keys inside, so you will have them with you at all times." The Princess attached the sash to her waist and returned the keys to their pocket. Then she clutched the book close to her heart. He continued, "The writings inside this book will give you understanding of your true identity, and the magnitude of all that has been bestowed upon you. You must then share the secrets with all of mankind."

"I will cherish it always," she replied with tears welling up in her eyes once again. Her thoughts now quickly turned to her unfounded resentment towards the King. "Thank You, and please thank King Elohim for me when You see Him."

"You can thank Him yourself," He replied reassuringly. He knew of Destiny's anger towards the King. He also knew of all her dreams and that the dreams carried messages that were explaining things to her. "Just look up and tell Him. He will hear you." Then He smiled.

"Thank You, King Elohim," she called, gazing up at the still cloudy, and darkened sky. "I am eternally grateful." Then she softly added, "I'm sorry dear King for being angry. I only saw things in my own perspective but now I know how vast and deep your love is for me and Mankind. It is more awesome than I ever imagined."

As she finished speaking, she felt her heart grow lighter and a burden from within lift from her. As she stood experiencing again an inner peace that passes understanding, she thought she saw in those same clouds the form of a snowy white bearded face with stars set in the middle of each eye, twinkling back at her.

Then the Prince took the book from her arms, and laid it on the bed, before taking her hands in His strong and scarred ones.
"I must go now and return to My Kingdom."
"Oh no!" she replied impulsively. "I thought...." her voice trailed off, as she didn't want to finish what she was going to say.

The Prince, knowing what she was thinking, replied, "It is not yet time for Me to take you away, but you must prepare for Our Wedding Day. You will also need to make ready the kingdom for the imperial celebration, so that all of Mankind will have been told of the great sacrifice that was made on their behalf and of My love for them. They then can choose to become part of our union," said the Prince.

The Royal Commission

All the land needs to be made aware of our regal wedding ceremony and banquet celebration, and as many as possible need to attend. All who hear and will come, need to be wearing a white linen wedding garment. Not one will be permitted to come in without a wedding garment," He continued.

"How shall I accomplish such a task?" asked the Princess feeling a bit overwhelmed at what was being asked of her.

"Make new spinning wheels for the kingdom, to prepare the garments," said the Prince. "You see, when your parents had the spinning wheels burned so you would not prick your finger on the spindle needle, they played right into Beelzebub's wicked plan."

"Oh, is that what I touched in the storage room?" said the Princess.

"Yes," He said. "There was only one that escaped destruction, only because it was hidden in storage since before your dedication. I tried to warn you not to touch it, but you did not listen." Destiny hung her head in shame, remembering that day.

"I did not know it was Your voice I heard," she admitted. The Prince lifted her head with His hands and looked into her eyes.

"From now on you will know My voice," He said, and kissed her forehead to enlighten her mind. Then He continued with His story. "Beelzebub knew that the day would come, when you would need the spinning wheels to make the garments. Hence, a decree must be issued throughout the land to lift the ban that was placed so many years ago. Let the proclamation go forth and let everyone make new spinning wheels. I will also send you many faithful servants to help make the garments. I will even send you loyal soldiers who will go into the highways and byways to bid all of Mankind to come in. No matter what you need, I will supply it!" exclaimed the Prince.

"I have also commissioned the Great and Powerful Paraclete to care for you until I come back. You must embrace His presence, for He will be your comforter until I return for you. He will protect you in the midst of any onslaught of the dark prince and his evil forces. You will not see Him as you did today, for He has the ability to change forms, depending on His purpose. Sometimes you will feel Him as a mighty wind, sometimes a blazing fire, other times as gentle as a dove, but you will always recognize Him when He comes," He reassured her.

Then Destiny nodded her head as she took His love-scarred hands in her own and looked up into her beloved's beautiful and sensitive face once more. She once again saw the image of herself in His dark piercing eyes, only this time she was not dreaming. She knew what she saw was the deep reflection of His heart shining through. He had thought of everything. She would rest securely in that.

The Departure

"I will do all that You ask of me," she vowed to Him. Then a deep sadness began rising within her as she became aware that He was leaving. The Prince, sensing the distress of her innermost feelings, wrapped His arms around her.

"When will I see You again?" she said, their embrace finally ending.

"I will visit you often as I did today, but in different ways. Do not forget, My love, even if you do not see Me actually standing before you, I will never leave you or forsake you." It was then she knew in her heart that it was time for Him to go.

White smoke appeared in the room and slowly began to thicken. Through it she could see that the Prince was beginning to fade away. She watched through tear filled eyes, as the last particles of His image finally all but disappeared into thin air.

"Until We are one," called the vanishing Bridegroom to His Bride, the smoke overtaking the last fragments of His image.

"Until We are one," the Bride called back to her Bridegroom. Then He was completely gone.

The Vision

Slowly, the atmosphere in the room began to change. The smoke disappeared, swept away by a cool breeze carrying a sweet fragrance upon it. The Princess dried her eyes and followed the aroma to the window of her chambers to look out at her new kingdom. It was the dawn of a new day, with evidence of the splendor of springtime surrounding her as far as her eyes could see. The dark and stormy cloud that had covered the kingdom for so long had dissipated. In its place was radiant sunshine, and the early morning sound of birds singing filled the air like music. The thorny fortress that had surrounded the castle had completely disappeared too. In its place had sprouted a marvelous show of beautiful flowers in full bloom. They dotted the hillsides with a kaleidoscope of color across the land.

Destiny took a deep breath of the refreshing air and thought of Him. His peace filled her being as she pondered His words to her.
As she sat at her window seat gazing out at the splendor of the kingdom that surrounded her, she suddenly began to see a heavenly vision. Her thoughts were captured by a foggy scene of herself riding on the back of a brilliant white stallion.

Slowly the fog in the atmosphere began to clear, and the vision unfolded.

She saw through the remaining mist that the stallion was being led by her valiant Prince, who was walking ahead of them. An angel carrying a torch was flying before them, lighting the way. She wasn't sure where they were going, but she knew she had entered a foreign world of some sort, at a time somewhere in the future. It reminded her of the City of Paradise she seemed to be viewing in the dream that she kept having about the bride and groom. Could the city she saw in the dream she kept having be the Everlasting Kingdom? Is this what the Prince meant when He said that He would visit her often? All these things she wondered to herself as they continued their journey,

Dawn finally began to break in this strange and wonderful land. All around them, Destiny could see a world of indescribable beauty, to which the Kingdom of Mankind paled in comparison. Trees and flowers adorned in colors she had never seen before lined the path beneath them, a street that was paved in gold. As the exquisite foliage waved their heads in the gentle breeze, music came from their leaves and petals, and blended together into a melodious tune. She could scarcely take in the majesty of all that she saw, when suddenly she realized she was gazing at the most magnificent sight of all, the palace of the Almighty Trinity.

Upon reaching the Celestial Castle, the Prince helped Destiny down from the back of His strong, white steed. As her feet touched the ground, her clothes were transformed into a glowing, white wedding gown. She looked with surprise and amazement at Emmanuel from behind the transparent veil that now covered her face. His traveling clothes had also been changed as well, into a royal white wedding robe fit for a supreme royal occasion, and upon His head was a radiant gold crown adorned in gemstones.

"Oh my!" she gasped. She now knew who the Couple was that she saw over and over in her dreams. She continued to watch the vision unfold as He smiled at her, then took her by the arm and led her through the castle doors that were opened for them by two angels. As they stepped inside, she could barely comprehend the glorious majesty of the palace. Never in all her life had she seen so many rooms embellished in gold.

She turned to express to Him how her heart was bursting with joy, but He was gone! The angel that had led them on the horse appeared reassuring her that all was fine and handed her an exquisite bouquet of fragrant pink and white roses and instructed her that it was time to walk into her destiny. She nodded in agreement as peace and excitement filled her heart at the same time. Down a shimmering corridor that shined with an iridescence like pearls, she walked the aisle, which eventually opened into the magnificent Throne Room of King Elohim.

An angelic orchestra playing instruments accompanied a choir of the heavenly beings filling the atmosphere with symphonic music. A host of cherubim and seraphim singing “O Come Let Us Adore Him”, nodded and smiled as she passed by.

COME
LET US
ADORE
HIM

A great multitude of sons and daughters from the land of time, the land which she represented, lined the sides of the glassy sea ahead of them. They were all wearing the white wedding garments and the sashes with the hidden keys. They were all part of the same union now.

Then Destiny saw her Prince appear between two large cloud formations of a majestic Lion and Lamb. He smiled as she walked toward Him as His lovely Bride now prepared without spot or wrinkle. The Prince extended His arm to His Destiny as united they walked across the water of the Glassy Sea, toward the emerald Throne and bowed before the King. Elohim arose from His throne and greeted the Bride of His Son with a loving embrace. With tears in His eyes, He had them join hands, and performed the imperial wedding ceremony that would now unite their two kingdoms forever. Shaded by the wings of the Almighty Paraclete who hovered over the great Throne, the couple exchanged their vows.

Glowing mist began to fill the air again as the Bridegroom Prince finally lifted the veil of His long, sought after, Bride and tenderly kissed her lips with the everlasting kiss that would end all time, and begin their reign through all eternity. Then the mist in the vision grew thicker, obscuring it until it totally disappeared altogether.

Secrets Revealed

Destiny was now back in her chambers, seated in her window seat once again. Stunned and amazed at all she had been through that day, she sat gazing out the window, unable to move for a long while from the spot she was sitting.

Then suddenly she remembered the book that the Prince had given her. Hurriedly, she got up and moved toward the bed where the book was lying. There, she reached into the pocket of the linen sash she was wearing and removed the two keys marked "Surrendered' and "Obedience."

Then sitting down on the bed, she placed the book on her lap. She stuck the first key into the keyhole and turned it. The book opened, and she saw that she was able to flip through its pages and read it, just like any other book, though the words and sentences talked about things that were beyond her comprehension.

"Why are both keys necessary if it only takes one to open the book?" she wondered out loud. She closed it again, and this time inserted the second key. Cautiously, she opened the book again and at first saw no immediate difference. Then she decided that before she woke up her kingdom, she better uncover the secrets hidden in this treasury of truth she held in her hands.

As she began to read the very first page, something unusual began to happen. The words of the book began to light up, as rays of light shown up through each sentence that she read. Excited by what she saw happening, Destiny continued on. The illuminated words she was reading now began to make sense to her. Questions that she has had all her life were finally being answered. Captivated by all she was now able to understand, the Princess read on and on.

Faith is Stirred

Far below the Princess' room, lying amongst the slumbering prisoners in the council chambers, Faith began to stir. She opened her eyes finally and sat up, looking around her in the morning light at all the sleeping bodies. Rubbing the sleep from her eyes and feeling a little dazed, she sat pondering the sight. How was it that she was the only one awake? Then suddenly, a thought came to her, and she knew in an instant what had happened.

"The Princess! She has awakened!" exclaimed Faith.

Faith and Destiny were such kindred spirits that what happened to one always seemed to affect the other. Feeling a little shaken, Faith got up and carefully stepped over the bodies. She excitedly made her way to the staircase and climbed up the tower leading to the Princess' chambers. There, she knocked on the door, with great expectation in her heart.

A bewildered Destiny cracked opened the door and peered out, only to find Faith smiling back at her.

"Faith!" she squealed with excitement." You have awakened!" The two women hugged, thrilled to see each other, and to at last be free from the wicked curse.

"Is the Prince still here?" asked Faith knowing Destiny would not be awake if He hadn't already visited her. The two women sat down on the bed as Destiny explained.

"No," replied the Princess, her eyes suddenly downfallen. "He is already gone." She was unable to hide her disappointment from her friend. Faith heard the sadness in her friend's voice and patted her hand to comfort her.

"What was He like?" inquired Faith, her eyes sparkling brightly.

"There's no other like Him," sighed Destiny. "He is a brave and mighty warrior, able to defeat Beelzebub, yet He is as gentle as a lamb. He has a love for me and for all of Mankind like I've never seen before. I could never put all that He is. When He spoke to me, His kind voice brought peace to my heart and calmed all my fears. He told me of His plan to make ready the entire kingdom for His return and our royal wedding celebration."

Faith listened with rapt attention as Destiny explained all that the Prince had commissioned her to do. She told her about the spinning wheels and the white sashes with the hidden keys. Then the Princess showed Faith the book the

Prince had given her and how the words on pages would light up after inserting both keys. Faith's eyes widened, astonished at what her friend shared with her. Her mouth rounded wordlessly when Destiny told her next about her heavenly vision and the royal commission.

"What are we waiting for? We must follow Prince Emmanuel's instructions and do His bidding," exclaimed an enthusiastic Faith, bouncing off the bed. "Just let me freshen up a little. I feel like I've been collecting dust for a thousand years. Then I'll be back to help you get started reviving the others."

"Yes," responded Destiny. "We'll get started together. I'll wait for you here," she said, following Faith to the door and closing it behind her as she left the room. The princess smiled to herself. She was so happy to have a friend like Faith.

The fragrance from the flowers outside her chamber window seemed to beckon the Princess to return to her window seat. So, she sat down once more, captured by the beautiful surroundings and thoughts of her Dream Come True.

Even though, she knew she could not be with her beloved Emmanuel this day, she realized she would be someday soon. For now, with His image in her heart, she would instead carry His love like the breeze had carried the flowers' fragrance, to the Kingdom of Mankind in the realm of time as we know it.

THE END

'My Beloved said to me,
"Arise my darling, my beau-
tiful one and come away for
behold the winter is past,
the rain is over and gone
and flowers have already
appeared on the earth. The
time of singing has come,
the time of the pruning of
the vine. The voice of the
turtledove has been heard
in our land.
Arise! Arise my darling my
beautiful one.
Arise and come!"

- Song of Solomon 2:10-12, NLT -

Epilogue

Our story has concluded and so dear traveler you have come to the end of your journey. I hope that on this quest for truth you have found spiritual treasures you were seeking for.

The map to the treasure in our story has directed your path to the place where "X" marks the spot. It is my prayer that the hidden buried treasure that all of us in the Kingdom of Mankind search for throughout our lives, has now been found by you as well. The hidden treasure is the love relationship between Prince of Peace and his Bride. The "X" that marks the spot is found in not one, but two places.

The first "X" is found on our hearts, but the second one, on the heart of Emmanuel the Great. Without His sacrificial love, we would be at the mercy of Beelzebub and separated from Our God forever. If you still haven't unlocked your heart and found Him to be your destiny your decision to make this so is very easy. It's only a prayer away.

To receive all the riches that Emmanuel, the lover of your soul has for you, you need only to use the keys that unlock the secrets to the Everlasting Kingdom. The keys are "Surrender" and

"Obedience".

If what I have shared further intrigues you, say this prayer, even out loud so you can hear yourself speak it.

Dear Lord and Prince,

I surrender my heart and my life to you today. Going my own way and doing my own thing has led me to a life of disappointment and despair. I, like the Princess Destiny in the story, have wrestled with the fact that I have never known my true identity and what I mean to you. You loved me so much you gave up your life by suffering and dying to free me from my sins. Please come now into my heart where "X" marks the spot. I want you to be my Destiny, and I want to be yours. Amen."

If you have sincerely prayed this prayer from your heart, your heart and His heart no longer are separate but one. Now the blessings of life eternal are yours, and you may enter your destiny as an heir to the Everlasting Kingdom.

About the Story

The Secrets of the Everlasting Kingdom is written as a allegory type story that takes the age-old story of "The Sleeping Beauty" and uncovers spiritual concepts that are hidden there. Then combined with elements of the biblical book of "The Song of Solomon," the story develops into the story of Jesus and His loving and caring relationship with His Bride the Church. He wants His Bride to have ears to hear His voice and eyes to see .We must learn to open the eyes of our heart to see and hear his direction, and then act in faith to carry out what He shows us to do.

One of the story centralizing themes is how the Church, called to be the light of mankind, has fallen asleep to its primary purpose. She has not put her full attention on pleasing her beloved Bridegroom or fulfilling the great commission of going into all the world and making disciples. As in the parable of the Sower, (Matt.13) the cares of this world, and the deceitfulness of riches, have been choking the Word from her very heart. This is symbolized in the story by the great fortress of briars that surrounds the castle. In many parts of the Earth, the Church is waking up.

May this story speak to the part of the Bride that is already aroused as well as the part that still slumbers.

Characters and Symbols in the Story

King Elohim- Represents in the story, God the Father, first person of the Trinity. Ancient of Days is another of His many titles.

Prince Emmanuel- Represents Jesus, Son of God, second person of the Trinity, Bridegroom of the Church

The Great Paraclete- Represents the Holy Spirit, third person of the Trinity, also referred as Comforter

Princess Destiny- represents the Church, Bride of Christ

The King and Queen of The Kingdom of Mankind- represent the rulers and authorities on earth, who somctimes look to God, but more and more only as an afterthought if at all. Our world is rapidly becoming completely humanistic, with men who look to solely to their own strength. In the beginning of the story, they prayed, and received more than an heir to the throne. The Church has been birthed through mankind and is betrothed to Jesus the Bridegroom. A sleeping Church dims her light, and therefore man is searching in the darkness for truth. She needs to be revived to a deep love relationship with her Savior.

Beelzebub- Represents Satan

Giants- Represents strongholds that hold people in bondage.

Other Symbols

The Seven Ornate Pitchers- Seven is the number that represents God. Each Color of the precious stones covering the pitcher is a color of the dust it pours out. They represent the symbolic meaning for each gift.

Rubies- the color red is symbolic of redemption. The gift of grace was obtained for us by the shedding of blood.

Amethyst-the gift of leadership is symbolized by this purple-colored stone, which denotes royalty. Amber- this yellow color represents serving as in the "Golden rule", which states, "Do unto others as you would have them do unto you." It also represents the glory of God.

Emerald- this green color symbolizes growth and wealth. Givers recognize the blessing there is in giving.

Sapphire-Blue is the color of heavenly illumination. It represents wisdom that comes from God. Agate- this grayish-brown color symbolizes humility. "He who is greatest among you is the servant of all." The gift of humility is given to those who understand this great truth.

Diamond – The seventh gift is in the diamond -

covered pitcher of prophecy. Prophecy when clear and pure, clarifies the purpose and plan of God for His people – the Church.

The Secrets of the Everlasting Kingdom Book- represents the Holy Bible in the story. Only those who possess the keys can understand its truths.

The Keys- there are two keys necessary to open the truths of the secrets of the Everlasting Kingdom.

Obedience alone can sometimes be an outward appearance. The story of the rich young ruler, who kept all the commandments, is an example of this. He sadly walked away from Jesus when He required more than he wanted to give. Surrendered Obedience requires the laying down of one's will and following what God wants you to do. The scarlet ribbon holding the keys together represents the blood sacrifice of our great Prince.

The Sash- Symbolic of the belt of truth (Eph.6:14). The waist is the area of the body considered to be the seat of emotions. The sash with the keys girded around the waist to protect the believer from being deceived by being led astray from making decisions based on our emotions, rather than God's guidance.

The White Garments- signifies those who believe and have been washed by the blood.
"Though your sins be as scarlet, they shall be

made white as snow." (Is.1: 18) More scriptures to follow in the next section of the book to explain this more.

The Spinning Wheel – The Spinning Wheel symbolizes an instrument that God has given to us to fulfill His purposes and destiny, yet some in the Church have minimized its importance. When this occurs, she then "falls asleep" to the purposes of God. The result is that the instrument is "hidden away" and not allowed to do its part in sharing the Kingdom of God. The Lord has shown us the "Spinning Wheel" of the Church is the Great Commission commonly known as evangelism. In many places, this instrument has been used incorrectly and even without the love and compassion of the Father. The result has been that evangelism many times is distained by the Church and set aside. Man's futile attempt to use God's tool his own way has been many times ineffective or unloving, and the world stands and mocks it. Jesus has come not to a dead Church or a sleeping Church, but a Bride that is awake to her destiny.

Scriptures Explain the Message of the Story

In this section, we will give some examples through scripture of some questions that you may have had while reading this story. Though the number of references for each topic could be lengthy, we've tried to narrow it down to just a few.

1) Does God use stories, and symbols to convey truths about His Kingdom to us?

"The disciples came to him and asked, "Why do you speak to the people in parables?" He replied, "Because the knowledge of the secrets of the Kingdom of Heaven has been given to you, but not to them." - Matt 13:10-11, NIV

"Jesus spoke all these things to the crowd in parables; he did not say anything to them without using a parable. So was fulfilled what was spoken through the prophet: "I will open my mouth in parables, I will utter things hidden since the creation of the world."- Matt 13:34-35, NIV

2) Has God promised us eternal life and is He sovereign over all the Earth?

"For God so loved the world that he gave his one and only Son, that whoever believes in him shall not perish but have eternal life." -John 3:16, NIV

" In the beginning God created the heavens and the earth."- Genesis1:1, NIV
"It is written: "As surely as I live,' says the Lord, 'every knee will bow before me; every tongue will acknowledge God.'-Romans 14:11, NIV
"Righteousness and justice are the foundation of your throne; love and faithfulness go before you." - Psalm 89:14, NIV

3) Was Jesus' sacrifice enough to bring about my salvation?

"Now this is eternal life: that they know you, the only true God, and Jesus Christ, whom you have sent. I have brought you glory on earth by finishing the work you gave me to do." - John 17:3-4, NIV

"If you declare with your mouth, "Jesus is Lord," and believe in your heart that God raised him from the dead, you will be saved." - Romans 10:9, NIV

"You see, at just the right time, when we were still powerless, Christ died for the ungodly. Very rarely will anyone die for a righteous person, though for a good person someone might possibly dare to die. But God demonstrates his own love for us in this: While we were still sinners, Christ died for us." - Romans 5:6-8, NIV

4) Is the Church really the Bride of Christ?

"The Spirit and the Bride say, "Come!" And let the one who hears say, "Come!" Let the one who is

thirsty come; and let the one who wishes take the free gift of the water of life."- Rev.22:17, NIV

"I saw the Holy City, the new Jerusalem, coming down out of heaven from God, prepared as a bride beautifully dressed for her husband."- Rev. 21:2, NIV

5) What do the wedding garments mean?

"But when the king came in to see the guests, he noticed a man there who was not wearing wedding clothes. He asked, 'How did you get in here without wedding clothes, friend?' The man was speechless. Then the king told the attendants, 'Tie him hand and foot, and throw him outside, into the darkness, where there will be weeping and gnashing of teeth.' "for many are invited but few are chosen." - Matthew 22:11-14, NIV

"I delight greatly in the LORD; my soul rejoices in my God. For he has clothed me with garments of salvation and arrayed me in a robe of his righteousness, as a bridegroom adorns his head like a priest, and as a bride adorns herself with her jewels." Isaiah 61:10, NIV

6) Can following the Bible's life-giving words bring me understanding to transform my life?

"Therefore, if anyone is in Christ, the new creation has come: The old has gone, the new is here!" - 2 Cor 5:17, NIV

"Your word is a lamp for my feet, a light on my path." - Psalm 119:105, NIV

"Jesus answered, "It is written: 'Man shall not live on bread alone, but by every word that proceeds from the mouth of God.'" - Luke 4:4, NIV

"The LORD is my shepherd, I lack nothing." - Psalm 23:1, NIV

7) Can I hear God's voice?

"My sheep listen to my voice; I know them, and they follow me. I give them eternal life, and they shall never perish; no one will snatch them out of my hand." - John 10:27-28, NIV

"For whatever is hidden is meant to be disclosed, and whatever is concealed is meant to be brought out into the open. If anyone has ears to hear, let them hear." "Consider carefully what you hear," he continued. "With the measure you use, it will be measured to you—and even more. Whoever has will be given more; whoever does not have, even what they have will be taken from them."
- Mark 4 :22-25, NIV

"Whether you turn to the right or to the left, your ears will hear a voice behind you, saying, "This is the way; walk in it." - Isaiah 30:21, NIV

8) Does God hear and answer my prayers?

"If my people, who are called by my name, will humble themselves and pray and seek my face and turn from their wicked ways, then I will hear from heaven, and I will forgive their sin and will heal their land." - 2 Chronicles 7:14, NIV

"Truly he is my rock and my salvation; he is my fortress; I will not be shaken. My salvation and my honor depend on God; he is my mighty rock, my refuge." - Psalm62:6-7, NIV

" But the LORD has become my fortress, and my God the rock in whom I take refuge."
Psalm 94:22, NIV

"No temptation has overtaken you except what is common to mankind. And God is faithful; he will not let you be tempted beyond what you can bear. But when you are tempted, he will also provide a way out so that you can endure it." -1 Cor.13:10, NIV

"I cried out to God for help; I cried out to God to hear me." - Psalm 77:1, NIV

Adult Group Questions

This story speaks about the Sovereignty of God and the eternal plan of salvation written from before the foundation of the world. Looking at the Sovereignty of God in our own lives let's consider these discussion points:

1.) Can you remember a time or event in your life when you saw the guiding hand of an Almighty God directing your path?

2) Amid the journey how did you feel?

3) Princess Destiny's curiosity caused her to continue past the heartfelt check she received from Prince Emmanuel. This happens to all of us at one time or another. Any time that you feel free to share of when the voice of the Holy Spirit arose in your heart but you either didn't understand it or didn't heed it?

4) To unlock the book *(Bible)* required two keys. What do you believe the two keys represent?

(It requires both to unlock the deeper meanings of the book. The names of the keys are Surrender and Obedience. Attached by a scarlet ribbon symbolic of the sacrifice of Prince Emmanuel and given by grace from the Father, these are the true essence of a relationship with the Lord.)

The Spinning Wheel represents an instrument that had a particular purpose in the destiny of mankind. But because of the work of the evil Beelzebub the very instrument that was to be used to create the wedding garments was distained and banished.

On a personal level, is there anything in your life that you felt was a clue to your destiny or calling but you "pricked your finger on" or an adverse circumstance caused you to stumble and "fall asleep"? Having identified the "Spinning Wheel", what place have you placed it in your life? Have you banished it to an insignificant place? Are you asleep to its effective use in the Kingdom? Or have you destroyed it entirely and in need of the grace of God's restoration of it?

5) As regards to the Church, the Spinning Wheel represents Evangelism. How do you really feel when you hear the term Evangelism? Could it be that the instrument of God to create the wedding garments for the wedding feast has been distained, ill-used, and set aside?

Children and Youth Discussion Questions

The God of the Universe has His hand on every aspect of our lives. It is His desire that all would come to the saving knowledge of Jesus Christ. The story shows what's happening in heaven and the scenes of what's happening on earth. It shows us God knows and sees all things. (The Window of Time through which He looks into this dimension.)

1) God always watches over us. Can you share a time when you felt God's presence watching over you and guiding or protecting you?

2) How did it make you feel about your relationship with God?

3) Princess Destiny's curiosity caused her great pain. She continued past the heartfelt check that told her to stop. We all have disregarded the Holy Spirit's warnings at one time or another. God's gift to us is conviction not condemnation. Can you remember a time when you disobeyed an authority like a parent, teacher, or someone else and how you felt?

4) To unlock Secrets of the Everlasting Kingdom required two keys. The names of the keys are Surrender and Obedience. How do these two keys unlock the deeper meaning of the book?

5.) In the story, the Spinning Wheel was in reality a gift that God had given to the people to create wedding garments for those in the kingdom so that all may attend the wedding feast of Prince Emmanuel and Princess Destiny. What gift or gifts do you think God has given you? (i.e. dance, singing, intellect, ability to work with your hands, drawing, painting, music, etc.)

6.) How do you see God using you and this gift to impact His kingdom here on the Earth?

Exploring the Characters' Reactions in the Story

1) Ignoring or not understanding the voice of The Prince, **Destiny** was led to a wrong choice. Can we make wrong choices for our destiny by not praying and seeking God for what He has for our lives? How do the choices we make affect others for good or bad ? *(Example:* The kingdom of the Princess)

2) How does obedience to The Prince bring life to the "kingdom" around us? *(Example:* **the sleeping people in the kingdom that need awakened***)*

4) **Princess Destiny's parents** lost hope speaks of losing endurance while waiting for years for answers to our prayers and then giving up. Their giving up caused the entire kingdom to fall asleep. What happens in our world when others see us persevere in faith and patience ? What are some ways we can do that and how does that bring life to those in our sphere of influence?

5) **Initially the King in Mankind** feared Beelzebub's intimidation by accusation (the enemy's favorite tool) of not being invited to Destiny's dedication. The King's fear permeated all those under his influence in his kingdom. As a result. they could not receive the prophetic word and they received from the angel but received the death curse given by Beelzebub instead. This caused them to live in fear instead.

How did making more wrong choice by destroying the spinning wheels and trying to handle matters in their own human strength cause them to fall into utter despair?

6) How does **faith** keep us focused on God ? In the story, Faith, not fear, would have focused the people on what God has said (the prophesy) during circumstances that look fearful and desperate. When we worry instead of pray and trust God for our outcome, what happens to us in our hearts, minds, and emotions? **Jesus asked, " when I come, will I find faith upon the earth?"*

7) **The kingdom of people** fell asleep and were overcome by the darkness. This allowed the enemy to raise up demonic strongholds (briars)imprisoning the entire kingdom. Does the enemy distract us today and if so in what ways?

8) After **Destiny** read "the Ancient Book" with BOTH keys, **"Faith"** was awakened first before anything else happened. What happens when we don't follow through with instructions we are given even in our everyday life?

At the end* **Destiny *told Faith about the Book and what she learned about the Prince and His Kingdom—Sometimes we need to speak the Word of God to our faith. *Just as* **Faith** *in the story needed to dust herself off to get ready to help Destiny revive the kingdom, we need to "dust" off our faith (from lack of use and being dormant).*

What are some ways we can do that ?

9) The entire story reveals the love of the **Prince** and His heart towards His Bride. We've watched lots of heroes saving their princesses in other stories we know. Why is this story different than those ?

About the Author

Carolyn Lacek is an author, illustrator, teacher and ministry leader, serving the body of Christ in different capacities for over thirty-five years. In her earlier years, she graduated from the Art Institute of Pittsburgh, and went to work for a local newspaper writing articles and illustrating editorial cartoons. She opened her own ceramics studio a few years later, where she taught lessons to women.
After meeting and marrying David Lacek who was in seminary at the time, she went on to join him in different ministries to churches in the Pittsburgh and surrounding areas as well. The couple eventually pastored their own congregation that they had for seven years. During this time they sometimes shared the pulpit teaming up to teach locally and internationally.

Carolyn had an art studio that was part of the church ministry and taught art lessons in various mediums to homeschool children and women. Her husband David, who wrote the question and answer section for this book, also established a church in Peru and helped with the ministry in several other churches abroad.

Her love for stories, writing and illustrating began in childhood sitting at her grandmother's feet and listening to the many stories that she wrote to entertain her grandchildren. She began writing when her own stories following in the footsteps of her grandmother. Although Grandma's stories were never published, Carolyn illustrated one of her stories when she was about nine years old.

As a homeschooling mom she continued to write while educating her two daughters. She went on to illustrate two self-published children's books for other authors. She also wrote articles for Jubilee News, a local Christian Publication. After closing their church in 2018, she taught K-12 art lessons in a local Christian school. Through the school's international outreach program, she taught online art classes to students in Liberia and China. In addition to writing and illustrating, Carolyn still enjoyed speaking and teaching at churches and group meetings. Her unique presentations of spiritual insights which she illustrates with easel art pastel drawings, is a God given gift for the edification of the body of Christ.

She and her husband David live in the South Hills of Pittsburgh with their daughter Angie. Their daughter Katie and husband Frank and daughter live in the Pittsburgh area as well.

NOTES

NOTES

NOTES

NOTES

Made in the USA
Monee, IL
20 October 2022

1c415e74-f69b-4fb3-9b89-a1d2d49dff7cR01